ASTRID & APOLLO

AND THE
STARRY CAMPOUT

BY
V.T. BIDANIA

ILLUSTRATED BY
DARA LASHIA LEE

PICTURE WINDOW BOOKS
a capstone imprint

Dedicated to my dad, Nao Vu Thao — V.T.B.

Astrid and Apollo is published by Picture Window Books, an imprint of Capstone.
1710 Roe Crest Drive
North Mankato, Minnesota 56003
www.capstonepub.com

Library of Congress Cataloging-in-Publication Data
Names: Bidania, V. T., author. | Lee, Dara Lashia, illustrator.
Title: Astrid and Apollo and the starry campout / by V. T. Bidania ; illustrations by Dara Lashia Lee.
Description: North Mankato, Minnesota : Picture Window Books, an imprint of Capstone [2020] | Series: Astrid and Apollo | Audience: Ages 6-8. | Summary: Astrid is anxious about her family's camping trip because she is afraid of the dark (and bears), but her twin Apollo is looking forward to the experience; and Astrid is doing okay, despite the bugs and the dark, until she hears the scratching outside the family's tent—but Astrid is determined not to let her father face the threat alone.
Identifiers: LCCN 2019057164 (print) | LCCN 2019057165 (ebook) | ISBN 9781515861225 (hardcover) | ISBN 9781515861317 (paperback) | ISBN 9781515861324 (adobe pdf)
Subjects: LCSH: Hmong American children—Juvenile fiction. | Hmong American families—Juvenile fiction. | Twins—Juvenile fiction. | Brothers and sisters—Juvenile fiction. | Camping—Juvenile fiction. | Fear of the dark—Juvenile fiction. | CYAC: Hmong Americans—Fiction. | Twins—Fiction. | Brothers and sisters—Fiction. | Camping—Fiction. | Fear of the dark—Fiction.
Classification: LCC PZ7.1.B5333 At 2020 (print) | LCC PZ7.1.B5333 (ebook) | DDC [Fic]—dc23
LC record available at https://lccn.loc.gov/2019057164
LC ebook record available at https://lccn.loc.gov/2019057165

Designer: Lori Bye

Design Elements: Shutterstock: Ingo Menhard, Yangxiong

Table of Contents

Hi, I'm Astrid. My twin brother is Apollo, and we were born in Minnesota. We live here with our mom, dad, and little sister, Eliana.

ASTRID GAO NOU

Hi, I'm Apollo! Our mom and dad were both born in Laos. They came to the United States when they were very young and grew up here.

APOLLO NOU KOU

MOM, DAD, AND ELIANA GAO CHEE

HMONG WORDS

gao (GOW)—girl; it is often placed in front of a girl's name. Hmong spelling: *nkauj*

Gao Chee (GOW chee)—shiny girl. Hmong spelling: *Nkauj Ci*

Gao Nou (GOW new)—sun girl. Hmong spelling: *Nkauj Hnub*

Hmong (MONG)—a group of people who came to the U.S. from Laos. Many Hmong from Laos now live in Minnesota. Hmong spelling: *Hmoob*

Nou Kou (NEW koo)—star. Hmong spelling: *Hnub Qub*

tou (TOO)—boy or son; it is often placed in front of a boy's name. Hmong spelling: *tub*

CHAPTER 1

Bright Enough

Astrid pushed the clothes to the side. She sat on the floor. Then she took a big breath. "Hiding in a dark closet is not fun," she said.

Astrid did not like the dark. She didn't like shadows. She felt worried when she couldn't see anything.

But she had her special glow-in-the-dark wand with her. The wand made her feel safe. She pressed the power button, and the wand turned on.

"Where are you, Astrid?" asked Apollo. Her twin brother stood outside the closet. She heard his voice through the door.

"Not in here!" said Astrid. She watched the lights from the wand glow onto the wall.

"Everyone's in the car already," Apollo said.

Astrid looked up at the door. "I said I'm not here!"

Her family was taking their first camping trip. Apollo had always wanted to go camping. He was so excited. Astrid was not.

"We're waiting for you," said Apollo.

"Guess you have to go without me," said Astrid.

"Hurry up so we can leave!" Apollo said.

Astrid made a face. "I don't want to go camping!"

"Why not?" Apollo asked. "Is it because of what Lily said?"

Astrid frowned.

Their cousin Lily just got back from camping. She told them she saw a bear playing in the trees near her camp! Lily said it was big . . . and mean.

Plus, Lily got fifty mosquito bites. At first, Astrid could not believe it. Then she counted them. It was exactly fifty bites!

Lily said the bathrooms were really smelly. The toilets didn't even flush! Every time she went near the bathroom, Lily pinched her nose. Her nose was all pink when she got back.

Astrid did not want to run into a big, mean bear. She did not want to get fifty mosquito bites. And she for sure did not want to use a toilet that didn't flush.

"Come out right now!" Apollo opened the closet door.

"Hey!" Astrid stood up. She dropped the wand.

Apollo laughed. "I knew you were in there!"

"Of course." Astrid put her hands on her hips. "You heard me talking."

Apollo peeked inside the closet. "Were you hiding so you don't have to go camping?"

Astrid made fists at her sides. "I was not hiding!" she said, even though she was.

Apollo saw the wand on the floor. The lights shined up at his face. "What are you doing, then?" he asked.

"I'm testing my glow-in-the-dark wand," Astrid said.

Astrid was not happy about sleeping outside. Sure, she would be in a tent with her family. But they would be in the dark. If the wand was really bright, Astrid would be able to see. Then she wouldn't have to think about shadows.

Astrid pointed at the wand. "Do you think it will give us enough light?" she said.

Apollo crossed his arms over his chest. "Enough light for what? Did Lily tell you a scary story about the dark too?"

"No, but I want to make sure our camp has a lot of light," said Astrid.

"It will!" Apollo said. "And if it does get really dark, you won't be alone. We'll all be together. You'll have such a good time, you won't even think about Lily! You can't believe her stories anyway."

Astrid knew that was true. Lily usually made things sound scarier than they were.

One time she said the new slide at the water park was 250 feet high. It turned out to be only twenty-five feet. Another time Lily said a giant gorilla broke out of his cage at the zoo. It turned out to be a baby chimp.

Still, Astrid couldn't help feeling worried.

"I know you'll like camping, Astrid," said Apollo. "Listen, maybe Mom packed egg rolls. We all love her egg rolls! We can eat them on the way to camp. Or we can eat them at the camp. We can sit by a campfire. It will be an adventure!"

An adventure sounded nice to Astrid. "Are you sure?" she said.

Apollo nodded.

"Astrid and Apollo, what's taking so long?" Mom called from downstairs.

Apollo took Astrid's arm. "Let's go! Camping's going to be *so* fun!"

CHAPTER 2

Amazing Egg Rolls

On the way to the campground, the family stopped for burgers and fries.

Dad got the food at the drive-through window. Mom passed it to Astrid and Apollo in the back seat.

"Here's your lunch," she said.

"Thanks." Astrid sighed, looking down at her burger. She had been hoping for egg rolls. "Mom, I wish we had egg rolls."

"I'm sorry. I didn't have time to make them this morning," Mom said.

Apollo looked at Astrid. He shrugged. Astrid shrugged back.

"Your egg rolls are the most amazing egg rolls in the whole world," said Astrid.

"It's true, Mom. They are really good," said Apollo.

Dad nodded. "I agree. They're the best."

Mom smiled. "Thank you. Packing for camping took a long time. I promise to make amazing egg rolls another time."

Astrid took a bite of her burger.

Her baby sister, Eliana, sat in the car seat next to her. Astrid gave one fry to Eliana. Eliana bit into the fry, then took a sip of her milk.

Apollo sat on the other side of Eliana. He stuffed a bunch of fries into his mouth. He made funny faces at her.

Eliana laughed so hard she spit up milk. Then she screamed so loud her face turned red.

"You're hurting my ears!" said Astrid.

Mom turned around. "Where did she learn to do that?"

"She sounds like a wild cat," said Dad. He rubbed the side of his head.

"Was someone screaming on one of your baby TV shows?" Apollo said with his mouth full.

Eliana laughed.

"No more screaming, please," Mom said to her. After that, Eliana was quiet.

The campground was three hours away. Astrid sat back and fell asleep. When she woke up, Dad was driving into the state park.

He checked them in at the office. Then he bought a pack of wood. "For the campfire," he said.

They drove on a winding road into the forest.

"Look at all those trees," said Apollo.

Eliana looked out the car window. "Trees," she said, but it sounded more like *cheese*.

The trees were tall and pretty. The sun was shining down through the leaves.

Astrid watched the forest carefully. She wondered, were bears hiding in there? Big, mean bears with sharp claws and sharp teeth?

She hoped not. She tried to keep thinking about what Apollo said. Camping was fun. Fun. FUN!

After a few minutes, Dad said, "There it is!" He turned off the road and parked. Everyone got out of the car.

The camp area had a picnic table, a fire pit, and a big, grassy open space.

Dad pointed at the grass. "That's where we put the tent."

Mom helped Eliana into her stroller. "We'll be right back. We're going to look for the water fountain."

Suddenly Eliana let out another scream. Everybody covered their ears.

Dad took the tent from the car. He spread it out on the grass. He handed a long, bendy pole to Astrid and Apollo.

Astrid held one end of the pole. Apollo held the other end.

Dad showed them loops on the outside of the tent. "Now stick the pole into these loops," he said to them.

Next Dad shoved metal pegs into the grass. He used a small hammer to pound the pegs into the ground.

Astrid and Apollo went to the car and got more tent poles. They put them through the tent loops.

Then the twins helped Dad stick the ends of the poles into the pegs.

The poles lifted the tent up high. Soon the tent was standing up like a little house.

Astrid looked up at the orange
and purple sky. The sun was setting.
She hurried to the car. She had to
get her glow-in-the-dark wand. But
when she opened the car door, the
wand wasn't there!

CHAPTER 3

Don't Look Down

"Oh no!" said Astrid. She remembered now. The wand was at home. She had dropped it on the closet floor. She forgot to pick it up!

Astrid saw Mom and Eliana coming back to the camp. She bit her lip.

Mom pushed Eliana's stroller over. "What's wrong?"

Astrid did not want to tell Mom that she forgot her wand.

She did not want to say she was scared of shadows, big, mean bears, or the smelly camp bathroom. She was afraid if she talked, she might cry.

Finally she said, "I don't want mosquito bites." It was a half lie.

"Don't worry," Mom said. "This park doesn't have mosquitos."

Astrid looked at her in surprise. "It doesn't?"

"That's why we came here," said Mom.

"Aren't mosquitos everywhere?" Apollo asked.

"A lot of bats live near this park. The bats eat all the mosquitos," said Dad.

No mosquitos? That would mean no mosquito bites! Astrid was so happy she wanted to shout, "Yes!"

Mom put her arm around Astrid. "Do you feel better now?"

Astrid nodded.

"Can you two help get water?" Mom asked.

She handed Astrid and Apollo two big water bottles. She pointed to a grassy trail. "Follow that to the road. Then go straight. The water fountain is at the end of the road. It's near the bathroom."

Uh-oh, Astrid thought. She was trying to forget about the bathroom. Now she felt like she needed to use it soon.

She and Apollo walked on the trail. They came to a dusty road. Some kids rode by on bikes. Their bike wheels made a crunchy sound on the dirt road.

They passed other tents. Smoke rose from fire pits. Campers grilled burgers and hot dogs.

The campers waved at Astrid and Apollo. They waved back.

Astrid saw another Hmong family. Two little boys sat on a bench with their dad. The dad was fixing the line on his fishing pole. The mom was smashing something in a bowl.

Astrid smelled shrimp paste. "She's making papaya salad," she said to Apollo.

"I was going to say that!" Apollo said. He pretended to smash something in a bowl too.

Astrid laughed.

Apollo pointed up ahead. "There's the water fountain."

Astrid saw it. The fountain was next to a small wooden building with a big door.

Apollo grinned. "That must be the bathroom."

He went first. When he came out, he said, "Don't look down!"

Astrid couldn't wait anymore, so she went in. She decided not to hold her nose. She didn't want it to turn pink. Instead, she did something else.

She held her breath the whole time. And she didn't look down.

She looked up, though. She saw skinny spiders on the wall. They were chasing ants! Flies and moths flew around the light above her. Big beetles hurried after small beetles by the window. They looked like they were biting each other!

Astrid was too busy holding her breath to be scared of them.

She squirted hand gel on her hands and ran outside.

Apollo was waiting by the fountain. "Let's fill the water bottles," he said. He held his bottle under the fountain.

Astrid turned it on. Water splashed onto Apollo.

He jumped back. "It's so cold!"

Apollo looked silly. He was shouting, hopping, and shaking off water. Astrid laughed.

When Apollo's bottle was full, Astrid turned off the water. "My turn!" she said. The twins traded spots.

Astrid moved back. She did not want to get splashed. When her bottle was full, the twins walked back toward the camp.

Astrid looked up. It was darker now. The sky was gold and red. It looked like Italian ice.

Apollo was watching the sky too. "We're far from the city. I bet the stars will be brighter here."

"I forgot about that!" Astrid smiled. She liked stars.

"See? Camping isn't bad, right?" said Apollo as they walked along the trail.

"Not *that* bad," said Astrid. She tried not to think about shadows coming out.

When they got back to the camp, Astrid and Apollo gave Mom the water. Dad passed around headlamps.

He set one lamp on top of Astrid's head. Then he turned it on. A bright light glowed onto the ground.

"You're the sun, so you get the brightest lamp," he said.

Dad was talking about Astrid's
Hmong name, *Gao Nou*. It means
"sun." He always told her she was
the brightest light in the family.

Astrid smiled. She didn't have her
glow-in-the-dark wand, but she had
this for now.

CHAPTER 4

Shiny Stars

Mom put two lanterns on the picnic table. Light shined all around. Astrid was glad it was bright.

Dad set some wood in the fire pit. He started a fire. The red flames grew bigger and bigger.

"That's cool, Dad!" said Apollo.

Eliana sat in her stroller. She pointed at the fire.

"Don't touch. Fire is very hot. Okay?" said Astrid.

Eliana pulled her arm back.

"Let's start making dinner," Mom said.

Dad poked the fire with a long stick. "Who wants to help with the chicken wings?"

"Me!" said Apollo.

"Can you help with the rice and pepper sauce?" Mom asked Astrid.

"Yes!" said Astrid.

Soon the fire was ready. Dad and Apollo put the chicken on the grill.

Mom gave Astrid packs of purple sticky rice. The rice was still warm because it had been cooked that morning. Astrid opened the rice packs. She put the rice on paper plates.

Next Mom took out the cutting board. Astrid handed her Thai chili peppers. Mom cut the peppers into little pieces. Astrid helped her mix them into a sauce.

Eliana reached for the pepper.

"No, it's spicy!" Mom said. She moved it away.

"Spicy," said Eliana, but it sounded more like *spies see*.

Dad and Apollo carefully turned over the chicken wings.

"I'm getting so hungry," said Apollo.

"Me too." Astrid rubbed her stomach.

Dad stuck a fork in the chicken. "It's almost ready."

"It smells good," said Mom.

The chicken reminded Astrid of Hmong Village Mall. "It smells like the barbecue shop at Hmong Village!" she said.

Going to Hmong Village was so fun. The small shopping mall was always filled with people. The busy shops had the best food and drinks.

Suddenly Astrid remembered her favorite drink.

She got up and ran to the car. Her small cooler was on the back seat. Astrid carried her small cooler back to the fire. She put it on the bench. Her sweet soybean drink was inside.

Astrid took out the drink. She saw Dad by the big cooler. He had a package of Hmong sausages.

"Is that for breakfast tomorrow?" she asked.

"This?" Dad handed the package to her. "Yes. We'll cook it in the morning."

"I can't wait!" Astrid loved Hmong sausages. They were spicy, crispy, and crunchy. They tasted so different from sausages at the regular grocery store.

"Dinner's ready!" Mom said.

Astrid quickly placed the sausages in her cooler. She put the cooler under the table.

Then she ate dinner under the stars. The stars were so pretty. They shined like tiny lights.

The twins dipped the chicken in the sauce. Mom and Dad poured the spicy sauce over their plates.

The chicken wings tasted so good. The purple sticky rice was soft. The pepper sauce was spicy, salty, and sour.

Mom pressed the rice into little balls. She fed it to Eliana with small bites of chicken.

Astrid looked around the campfire. Her parents were talking and smiling. Apollo and Eliana were laughing.

Astrid did not want to worry about shadows anymore. She just felt happy to be with her family.

After dinner, everyone was full. They sat by the fire.

"See the stars?" said Dad. He was holding Eliana in his lap.

Eliana stared up at the starry sky.

"They are very shiny, just like you." Mom tapped Eliana's nose.

"Me?" said Eliana.

"Your Hmong name is *Gao Chee*. It means 'shiny!'" said Astrid.

"Don't forget those shiny stars are *me*!" said Apollo, laughing.

"You?" said Eliana.

"Apollo's Hmong name is *Nou Kou*. That means 'star!'" Astrid said.

Eliana nodded. Then she yawned.

"And that means it's time for bed," said Mom.

Everyone helped clean up. Then Mom handed out toothbrushes. They all brushed their teeth outside.

Then they took turns walking to the bathroom to change. First Mom and Astrid went. Then Dad and Apollo went. They used their headlamps to light the way.

Campers were still awake.
Families stood by the water fountain.
Kids played by the road.

Astrid watched everyone around her. Even though it was night, she didn't feel scared.

When they were all in their pajamas, Mom said it was time to get in the tent. Eliana was already in her playpen. She was sound asleep. They crawled into their sleeping bags.

"You can turn off your headlamps," Dad said.

Astrid knew it would be dark. But she felt safe in the tent. She turned off her headlamp.

"Good night, Astrid and Apollo," Mom and Dad said together.

"Good night, Mom and Dad,"
they both said.

Astrid smiled. She zipped up her
sleeping bag. She snuggled into it
and closed her eyes. That's when she
heard a scratching noise outside.

CHAPTER 5

Coo-Coons

Astrid's eyes opened wide. She stayed very still.

"What's that sound?" Mom said in the dark.

Is it a bear? Astrid wondered.

Astrid wished she had her glow-in-the-dark wand. No, she wished she was home. She wished she was inside her house, with the doors locked!

The scratching grew louder. Something was moving around.

It was right outside the tent.

Dad got out of his sleeping bag. "I need light," he said.

Apollo handed Dad his headlamp. Dad turned it on. It wasn't as bright as Astrid's. Dad moved the dull light across the window. Then he stepped over to the tent entrance and unzipped the flap.

He was going outside!

Astrid's heart pounded. She could not let a big, mean bear with sharp claws and sharp teeth get her dad.

"Wait!" she said.

Astrid jumped up from her sleeping bag.

She put on her headlamp. Then she hurried after Dad.

"I'm going too!" said Apollo.

"Be careful!" Mom whispered.

Astrid and Apollo followed Dad outside.

The night was so dark. Only a soft glow came from Dad's headlamp. A quiet wind blew past the trees. Crickets chirped a loud song.

Dad turned to Astrid and Apollo. He pointed to the left. This meant he would go left.

Astrid and Apollo nodded. They pointed to the right.

All of a sudden, Astrid heard the scratching noise again. It was too dark to see anything.

She turned on her headlamp. A
white light splashed onto the grass.
Then she saw it.
Two small eyes glowed up at her.
Behind those eyes were more eyes.

It looked like a field of tiny, shiny Christmas lights.

It wasn't a bear! It was a group of raccoons. She knew it by the masks around their eyes and the stripes on their tails. She remembered learning about raccoons at school. They didn't like bright lights *or* loud noises.

Astrid aimed her headlamp straight at the raccoons. Right at that moment, Eliana woke up inside the tent and screamed.

The raccoons took off.

Apollo jumped up and down. "You saved us, Astrid!"

Dad ran over. "Good job! You used your light to scare them away!"

"It was Eliana's scream too!" Astrid said.

"Is everything okay?" Mom asked through the tent window. "Was it a bear?"

Dad, Apollo, and Astrid laughed.

Dad opened the tent flap. They stepped back inside. "Raccoons," he said. He zipped the tent closed.

"Coo-coons," said Eliana.

"They were staring at us with beady little eyes. Then Astrid scared them off with her light!" Apollo said.

"She was very brave." Dad put his hand on Astrid's shoulder. "We are lucky we have Astrid to protect us."

"You should have seen her, Mom!" said Apollo.

"I'm proud of you," Mom said. She patted Astrid's back and kissed her head.

"Thanks," Astrid said. She smiled.

It was dark, but she felt like everything was full of light.

"Back to bed, everybody," said Mom.

It was hard to calm down after that. Astrid didn't know how or when, but she finally fell asleep.

In the morning, she woke up to birds chirping. The sun was shining in through the top of the tent. The wind blew fresh air into the window.

Astrid got up and ran outside. She saw little paw prints on her cooler. She opened the lid.

The Hmong sausages were gone.

"Always remember to lock coolers in the car," said Dad.

"Sorry," Astrid said. "I forgot it was under the table."

"It's okay. Remember for next time," Dad said.

Astrid nodded. "I won't forget!" She sighed. "Now we don't have breakfast."

"Well, maybe we do," said Mom. She opened the big cooler. She pulled out a large plastic bag.

"Is that egg roll filling?" said Apollo.

Mom nodded. Then she took out a flat square package.

"Egg roll wrappers!" Astrid said.

Mom smiled. "You saved our family from a raccoon attack. So we will cook amazing egg rolls for you!"

Astrid hugged Mom. "Thank you!"

Eliana watched them. Then she opened her mouth wide to scream.

"No!" said Dad. He quickly covered it with his hand.

Then everyone laughed.

Astrid looked at Apollo. He gave her a big grin.

Astrid smiled back. She thought about everything that had happened at camp.

She had run into raccoons, but she did not run into a bear. She saw bugs biting each other, but she did not get mosquito bites. She held her breath in the bathroom, and she did not smell anything stinky.

Instead, she ate dinner under shining stars. She was brave. She had protected her family. She was not afraid to be in the dark anymore.

Astrid didn't need her glow-in-the-dark wand after all. She'd had an adventure, just like Apollo said she would. He was right. Camping *was* fun!

- Hmong people first lived in southern China. Many of them moved to Southeast Asia in the 1800s. Some Hmong decided to stay in the country of Laos (pronounced *LAH-ohs*).

LAOS

- In the 1950s, a war called the Vietnam War started in Southeast Asia. The United States joined this war. They asked the Hmong in Laos to help them. When the U.S. lost the war, Hmong people had to leave Laos.

- After 1975, many Hmong came to the U.S. as refugees. Refugees are people who escape from their country to find a new, safe place to live. Today, Minnesota is home to around 85,000 Hmong.

- Many Hmong American families enjoy outdoor activities like camping, boating, and fishing.

egg rolls—crunchy, fried rolls made of ground meat, vermicelli noodles, and vegetables that are wrapped in rice paper.

Hmong sausages—crispy, crunchy sausages made of pork, pepper, and other spices. Some Hmong sausages are spicy and some are not.

papaya salad—a sour, spicy salad made of papaya (that is not yet ripe), tomatoes, garlic, lime, shrimp paste, fish sauce, and fresh pepper. The ingredients are smashed together using a mortar and pestle.

pepper sauce—a very spicy sauce made with chopped Thai chili peppers, lime, and fish sauce. It is used as a dip for meat.

soybean drink—a drink made of sweetened soy milk. Soybean drinks are a favorite of many Hmong children. They can be found in nearly every Asian grocery store!

sticky rice—soft, sticky rice that kids like to smush into little balls and eat by hand. The rice is a light cream or purple color.

GLOSSARY

adventure (ad-VEN-chur)—an exciting experience

beady (BEE-dee)—small, round, and shiny

headlamp (HED-lamp)—a light worn on the head

mosquito (muh-SKEE-toh)—a small insect that bites animals and humans and sucks their blood

papaya (puh-PAH-yuh)—a sweet fruit that grows on a tropical tree

shiny (SHYE-nee)—filled with light

shrug (SHRUHG)—to raise and lower your shoulders to show that you don't know or don't care about something

spicy (SPYE-see)—having lots of flavor

Thai chili pepper (TYE CHILL-ee PEP-er)— a hot pepper that is used in cooking

wand (WAHND)—a thin rod, especially one used by magicians

wrapper (RAP-ur)—a thin material that covers or protects something

1. Astrid was scared to go camping. Were you ever scared of something like she was? Did you tell anyone? Were you glad you told them?

2. The stars at the campground were so bright. Why? Have you ever seen very bright stars? Where were you?

3. Apollo knew Astrid was nervous about camping. What did he say to help her? Have you ever helped someone like this? Discuss what you said or did.

1. What was Astrid afraid of at camp? Make a list of things that made her scared. Draw a picture of one of those things.

2. Astrid thought a bear was outside the tent. Even though she was very scared, she ran outside to protect her dad. Write about a time when you were brave and faced one of your fears.

3. After Astrid went to sleep, she heard a noise. Did you ever hear a scary noise at night? Write about the noise and what happened after it woke you up.

ABOUT THE AUTHOR

V.T. Bidania was born in Laos and grew up in St. Paul, Minnesota. She spent most of her childhood writing stories, and now that she's an adult, she is thrilled to be writing stories for children. She has an MFA in creative writing from The New School and is a recipient of the Loft Literary Center's Mirrors and Windows Fellowship. She lives outside of the Twin Cities with her family.

ABOUT THE ILLUSTRATOR

Dara Lashia Lee is a Hmong American illustrator based in the Twin Cities in Minnesota. She utilizes digital media to create semi-realistic illustrations ranging from Japanese anime to western cartoon styles. Her Hmong-inspired illustrations were displayed at the Qhia Dab Neeg (Storytelling) touring exhibit from 2015 to 2018. When she's not drawing, she likes to travel, take silly photos of her cat, and drink bubble tea.